Snipp, Snapp, Snurr
LEARN TO SWIM

MAJ LINDMAN

ALBERT WHITMAN & COMPANY
Morton Grove, Illinois

The Snipp, Snapp, Snurr Books
Snipp, Snapp, Snurr and the Buttered Bread
Snipp, Snapp, Snurr and the Gingerbread
Snipp, Snapp, Snurr and the Red Shoes
Snipp, Snapp, Snurr Learn to Swim

The Flicka, Ricka, Dicka Books
Flicka, Ricka, Dicka and the Little Dog
Flicka, Ricka, Dicka and the New Dotted Dresses
Flicka, Ricka, Dicka and the Three Kittens
Flicka, Ricka, Dicka Bake a Cake

Library of Congress Cataloging-in-Publication Data
Lindman, Maj.
Snipp, Snapp, Snurr learn to swim / Maj Lindman.
p.   cm.
Summary: On a summer vacation at the seashore,
three little Swedish boys finally learn to swim well enough
to place first, second, and third in the children's races.
ISBN 0-8075-7506-2
[1. Brothers—Fiction. 2. Seashore—Fiction.
3. Swimming—Fiction. 4. Sweden—Fiction.] I. Title.
PZ7.L659Sr 1995   94-37263
[Fic]—dc20   CIP
                                               AC

The text is set in 23' Futura Book
and 12' Bookman Light Italic.

A note to grownups
In this story, the characters are not wearing personal flotation devices or practicing some of the other water safety measures we now consider essential. While reading this book with children, you may want to use the story as a springboard to discuss safety around water and boats.

A Snipp, Snapp, Snurr Book

Up the hill was the little red cottage.

It was summer in Sweden. Father was going on a long business trip. Mother was going with him.

She had said, "I feel perfectly safe to let our boys go with Nanny to the seashore. She took me to the same little red cottage when I was their age."

On the day Mother and Father left, Snipp, Snapp, and Snurr went with Nanny to the cottage at the seashore.

They rode the train all morning. At noon they got off. Up the hill was the little red cottage.

Nanny opened the little red cottage, and they all went in.

While Nanny fixed lunch, the boys unpacked and put on their shorts and summer shirts.

After lunch they ran down to the beach to find Nick Larson and his father. The Larsons lived close by and went fishing every day.

Mr. Larson and Nick were away. By the house, fishing nets were hanging up to dry. Nick's cat, Cuddles, came toward the boys. Snurr found little fish caught in the nets and gave them to her to eat.

Snurr gave the cat little fish to eat.

Early the next morning Snipp, Snapp, and Snurr again went to find the Larsons.

Nick and Mr. Larson were standing near their boat. "Hi, boys," Nick called. "We're very glad to see you. Hop in with me, all of you. I'm just going out to drop the nets."

Mr. Larson helped them into the boat. Nick took the oars as Mr. Larson pushed the boat into the water.

Snipp and Snapp sat down.

But Snurr began to jump from one side of the boat to the other. The boat tipped, and Snurr fell in!

Nick knew what to do. "Take my oar, Snurr," he said. "Hold on tight, and I'll pull you aboard. Snipp and Snapp, you must sit down!"

"Take my oar, Snurr," he said.

Nick helped Snurr into the boat. "I have to drop the nets, Snurr," he said, "or I'd take you back right away. You boys should learn to swim if you want to have fun at the seashore.

"Never jump around in a boat. That makes it tip. Now, each of you must sit very still."

Nick rowed out to sea, dropped the nets, and rowed back quickly.

Nanny was frightened when she heard why Snurr was wet from head to foot. And she was cross.

"You boys stay close to me on this beach," she said, "and play with your sailboats. I'll do my washing right here where I can watch you. Each one of you should learn to swim."

"You boys stay close to me and play with your sailboats."

When Nanny had done her washing, she hung the clothes on the line to dry.

Her big green tub was empty. "Let's pretend Nanny's tub is a boat," said Snipp. "Water can't hurt it." The three little boys pushed and dragged the tub down to the shore.

"Let's push it into the water," said Snurr. "It will float just like a real boat." They gave the tub a strong push, and it slipped into the water.

"We're barefoot," said Snapp, "so we can wade in. Climb in with me, Snipp."

They gave the tub a strong push.

Snipp and Snapp got into the big tub. Snurr stood in the water near them.

There was a light breeze. Behind them was the wide blue sea.

Snapp stood up. "This is our boat!" he cried. "I'm the captain!"

Suddenly the breeze grew strong. It began to blow the green tub away from shore. Then Snapp lost his balance and sat down fast in the tub.

Snipp stood waving his arms and smiling as he said, "Ship ahoy!"

Snurr stood on the beach. He watched the make-believe boat floating out to sea. The strong breeze kept right on blowing.

Snapp sat down fast in the tub.

Snipp sat down. He and Snapp weren't smiling anymore.

Snurr saw that the tub was moving farther and farther out to sea. Suddenly he knew he could no longer wade out to it. He called to them, "Hold on! I'll get Nanny to help."

Nanny had just hung her last clean sheet on the line when Snurr shouted, "Oh, Nanny! Snipp and Snapp are floating away!"

When she saw Snipp and Snapp so far away, Nanny cried, "Oh Snurr, I can't swim! Whatever can we do?"

Snurr looked at Nanny.

"Whatever can we do?"

Oh, I know, Nanny," Snurr answered. "I will find Nick. I'll run as fast as I can to get him. He'll help us."

Off he ran very fast.

Nick was at home mending his fishing nets. Snurr was out of breath as he ran up. "Nick," he cried, "come with me quickly! Snipp and Snapp are floating away in Nanny's green washtub. We were playing it was a boat."

Nick jumped up. "I'll get my boat, and we'll go after them right now!" he shouted.

Off he ran very fast.

They slid the boat down the beach. Nick helped Snurr into the boat. He used one oar to push it into the water.

Then Nick got in and began to row with long, even strokes.

Snurr waved to Snipp and Snapp in the tub. "Don't be afraid!" he called to them. "We are coming!"

Nick and Snurr soon reached the boys. Nick helped them into the boat.

He asked Snapp to hold onto the green tub. Then he rowed them all to shore.

"Don't be afraid!" he called. *"We are coming!"*

Nanny hugged the boys. Then she scolded them.

Nick said, "I want to give them swimming lessons. May they put on their swimming trunks now?"

"Yes," Nanny answered. "I won't ever be happy until you teach them how to swim." She sent them into the cottage to put on their swimming trunks.

First, Nick showed them how to hold their breath under water. They stayed in shallow water close to the beach.

Another day, he taught them how to do the back float.

He taught them how to dog-paddle, too.

After many more lessons he said, "Now you may swim in deep water. Jump off the dock. Don't be afraid."

Nick taught them how to dog-paddle.

All three boys jumped into the deep water, then swam back to Nick.

"You boys swim just like three big fish," Nick said proudly.

Nanny said, "What a surprise you will give Mother and Father when they see you."

One fine morning Mother and Father arrived. The boys said, "Let's all go for a swim." They could hardly keep their big secret.

"All right," Mother said. "But keep away from the dock. The water is too deep for you there."

"We're not afraid," said Snapp. Splash! In went Snipp. Splash! In went Snapp. Splash! In went Snurr. They swam back to shore.

"How wonderful!" said Mother and Father. "What a surprise!"

"Let's all go for a swim."

A week later Father said, "There will be a swimming contest for children today. You may enter it if you like. You are to show the judge just how well you can swim."

At two o'clock the boys went with Mother, Father, Nick, and Nanny to a pretty bay.

All the children started from a point of land in the bay and swam to shore.

Snipp reached the shore first. Next came Snapp, then Snurr and the rest of the children. The judge laid a crown of green leaves on the head of each brother.

Father said, "Thank you very much, Nick. The boys will never forget their swimming teacher."

Snipp reached the shore first.